THE WEATHER CAT

Helen Cresswell

Illustrated by Barbara Walker

GALLERY BOOKS
An Imprint of W. H. Smith Publishers Inc.
112 Madison Avenue
New York City 10016

It was summer vacation.
Naomi and Otis were upstairs, helping their
mother make the beds.
They heard a noise downstairs.
"There's someone downstairs," said Naomi.
"In the kitchen."

"Go down and see," her mom said.
"It's probably Mr. Briggs. I'll be down in a minute."

Naomi went downstairs and into the kitchen.
There, rolling a spool of thread across the floor, was
a small tabby cat.

Naomi looked at the cat.
The cat looked back at Naomi.
"Hello, Mr. Briggs!" said Naomi.
"Mom says she'll be down in a minute."
The tabby cat went back to its game and the spool of
thread went back and forth.
Then Naomi gave the spool a kick.
The cat liked that. His tail twitched.
He crouched and sprang.

Naomi's mom came in.
"What's this?" said her mom.
"Mr. Briggs and I are playing soccer,"
Naomi told her.
"He's good at it!"
Now Otis came in, too.
"That's not Mr. Briggs!" he said.
"Yes it is," Naomi told him. "Another
Mr. Briggs."

Naomi got a carton of milk and a saucer.
"Would you like some milk, Mr. Briggs?"
she asked.
"It's half time!"
The cat purred.
"You see," said Naomi. "It *is* his name!"

Just then the real Mr. Briggs came in.
He had come to put in a new window pane.
"What's this?" he asked.
"I didn't know you had a cat."
"We didn't have one yesterday," Naomi told
him, "but today we do. His name is Mr. Briggs.
Same as you."
"That's strange!" said Mr. Briggs.

At dinnertime one Mr. Briggs went home.
The other stayed, and had some tuna fish and drank
two saucers of milk.
You can guess which did which.

One Mr. Briggs stayed all afternoon.
He curled himself up on the window sill.
He was still there when Dad came home.
"Can he stay?" Naomi asked.
"I think he likes it here," said Otis.
"If he did have a home already, he'd go
there I suppose," said Mom.
"He can stay if he likes," said Dad.

Mr. Briggs did like.

The next day Naomi found an old white plate and a white bowl.

Around the rim she painted the name Mr. Briggs in black paint.

Now Mr. Briggs had really come to stay.

Every morning Naomi came down and let him out.
Mr. Briggs would drink a saucer of milk, and then
go out into the yard.
After a week or two, Naomi began to notice
something.

If it was nice, Mr. Briggs would go and lie on top of the shed.
He was looking for birds.

If it was nice but cold, he would lie inside the shed.
He lay very still behind the push broom.
He was looking for mice and spiders.

But if it was wet, Mr. Briggs would soon come back
into the house.
He came in on tiptoe, so as not to get his feet wet.
Then he went into the closet under the stairs
and slept all morning.

Then Naomi noticed something else.
On some days Mr. Briggs would come and lie in his
closet even when it was nice.
On the days when he did that, it always *did*
rain, later on.

"Mr. Briggs is a weather cat!" Naomi told her
mom one day.
"He always knows when it's going to rain."
Mom was busy hanging out the wash.
"It isn't going to rain today," she said.
"Yes it is," Otis told her. "Mr. Briggs is under
the stairs."

Their mom laughed and went back inside.
Not long after, it began to rain. It poured.
Everyone ran out to take in the wash.
"I told you!" Naomi cried. "Mr. Briggs is a
weather cat!"

After that, they all took notice of what
Mr. Briggs did.
"He's on top of the shed today," Naomi's dad
would say.
"No need to take my umbrella to work!"
Or "He's inside the shed—better dress warm!"

The family would wait to see what Mr. Briggs did
every morning.
If he lay on top of the shed, Mom had a wash day.

But if he went into his closet, she said, "Better wait till tomorrow. Mr. Briggs is under the stairs."

One Saturday it was very nice weather, but
Mr. Briggs went under the stairs.
"That's funny!" Naomi said.
"It doesn't look a bit like rain."
"There'll be no washing today," said her dad.
"Mr. Briggs is never wrong."

At dinnertime Mr. Briggs was still in his
closet. And there hadn't been a drop of rain. Not
a single drop.
Naomi and Otis went and looked under the stairs.
There lay Mr. Briggs looking up at them.

And there, at his side, lay one, two, three, four
little kittens.
"Mom! Dad!" yelled the children.
"Come and look!"

Mom and Dad ran to look in the closet.

Now the tabby cat is called Mrs. Briggs, and has four weather kittens.
On nice days they lie on the roof of the shed, looking for birds.

On cold days they lie inside the shed, looking for mice and spiders.
And on wet days, they sleep in the closet under the stairs.

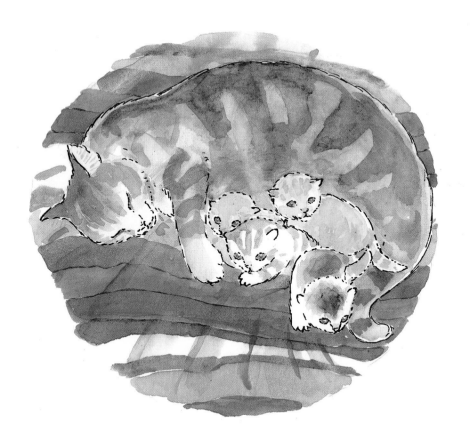

Soon Naomi and Otis will be giving the
kittens away.
Does anyone want a weather cat?

First published in the United Kingdom in 1989 by William Collins Sons and Co. Ltd. This edition first published in the United States in 1989 by Gallery Books, an imprint of W.H. Smith Publishers, Inc., 112 Madison Avenue, New York, New York 10016. Produced for Gallery Books by Joshua Morris Publishing, Inc. in association with William Collins Sons and Co. Ltd. Text copyright © 1989 Helen Cresswell. Illustrations copyright © 1989 Barbara Walker. All rights reserved. ISBN 0-8317-4453-7 Printed in Hong Kong.